Spike

Roary

Clawdie

For Juniper
-P.H.

For Eva,
Love Dad x
-D.G.

tiger tales

5 River Road, Suite 128, Wilton, CT 06897
Published in the United States 2021
Text by Patricia Hegarty
Text copyright © 2021 Caterpillar Books Ltd.
Illustrations copyright © 2021 Dean Gray
ISBN-13: 978-1-68010-280-2
ISBN-10: 1-68010-280-X
Printed in China
CPB/2800/1886/0621
2 4 6 8 10 9 7 5 3 1

www.tigertalesbooks.com

The TINYSAURS Send Love

by
Patricia Hegarty

tiger tales

Illustrated by
Dean Gray

It's that special time of year again,
when love should fill the air.
But where are the hearts and flowers?
There's no love anywhere!

"There's a problem here," says Clawdie,
"and *I* think we can all agree...."

Hmm...what are the Tinysaurs missing?
Roary knows what it might be!

Roary races to check the mailbox,
and is met with a sorry sight:

No letters or cards for anyone —
something is just not right.

The Tinysaurs
start to investigate

and discover
a worrying tale.

"There must be
something we can do!"
says Clawdie with a frown.

"Maybe we can make some gifts
for everyone in town!"

"Why don't we give out balloons?" cries Spike. "Something everybody likes!"

POP!

But as soon as he has blown them up, they pop on all his spikes!

Clawdie rushes to the kitchen —
she really likes to bake,
and what says "*I love you*" better
than a yummy homemade cake?

Meanwhile, Roary is in the backyard,
and he has been thinking, too —

I'll pick some flowers for everyone:
"With love from me to you!"

But their efforts have
been a disaster —
Spike's balloons have all
popped one by one,

Roary's flowers
are quickly drooping,

and Clawdie's
cake is overdone.

"This just isn't working!" cries Clawdie,
"though we're doing the best that we can.

plan,
plan, plan!

We will all need to work together —
I think that I have a new plan!"

The Tinysaurs
leap into action.

There's a lot of
work to be done;

cutting and
drawing and coloring —

now, the delivery should be fun....

Spike has put on his in-line skates and delivers the cards with speed. He makes a great mail carrier — satisfaction guaranteed!

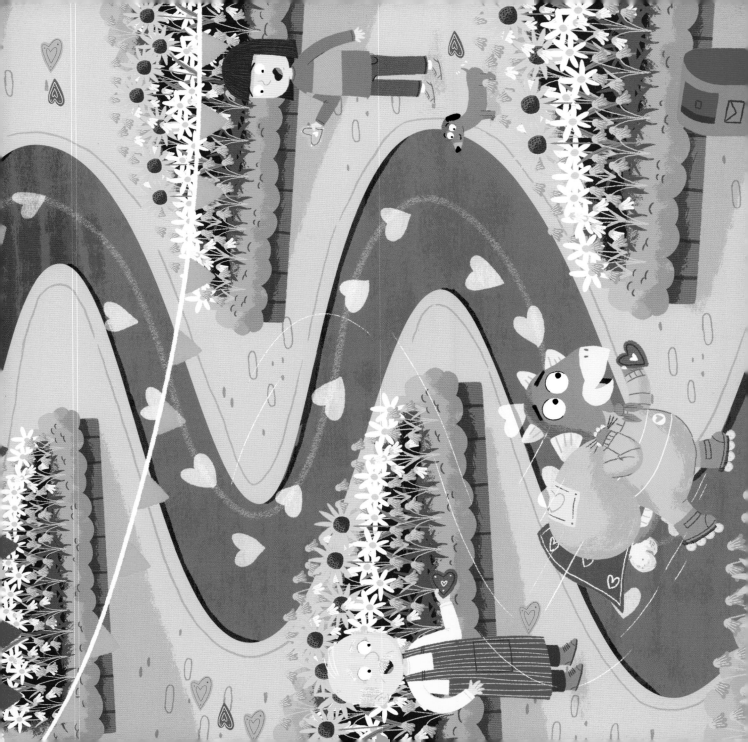

So the special cards of friendship
are delivered to countless doors,
and neighbors all smile at the message:
"With love from the Tinysaurs."

Everyone joins in the celebration —
it's buzzing in the town square.
As people all gather together,
love and friendship fill the air.

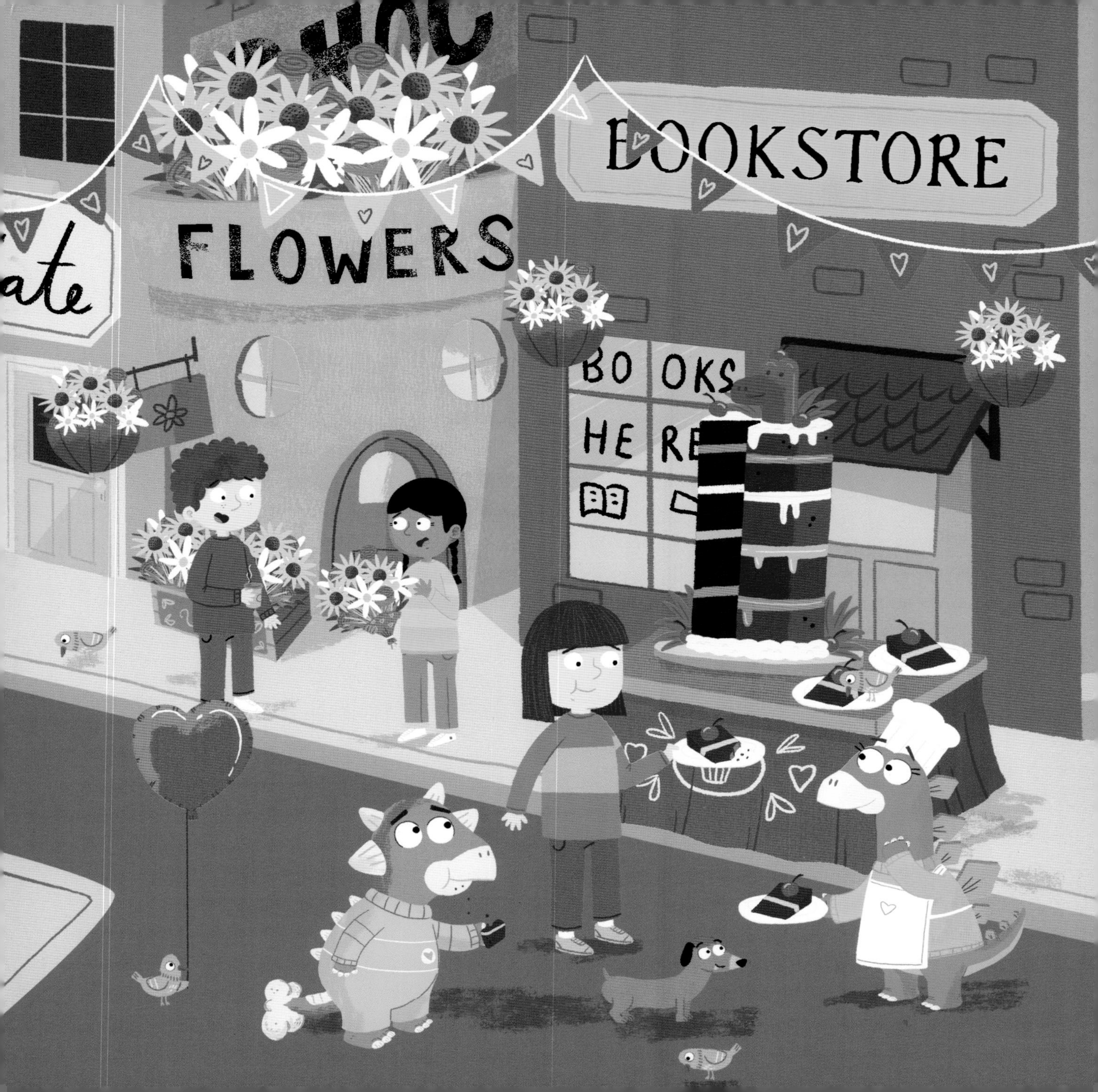

ate
FLOWERS
BOOKSTORE
BO OKS
HE RE

At the end of their adventure,
the Tinysaurs have agreed:
when it comes to friends and family,
love is all you need.